For Sam and Anna

Tundra Books, an imprint of Penguin Random House Canada Young Readers, a division of Penguin Random House of Canada Limited

Library and Archives Canada Cataloguing in Publication

Title: Wheels, no wheels / Shannon McNeill.
Names: McNeill, Shannon, 1970- author, illustrator.
Identifiers: Canadiana (print) 20210215488 | Canadiana (ebook) 20210215496 |
ISBN 9780735270374 (hardcover) | ISBN 9780735270381 (EPUB)
Classification: LCC PZ7.1.M46 Whe 2022 | DDC j813/.6—dc23

Published simultaneously in the United States of America by Tundra Books of Northern New York, an imprint of Penguin Random House Canada Young Readers, a division of Penguin Random House of Canada Limited

Library of Congress Control Number: 2021938649

Edited by Samantha Swenson
Designed by Jennifer Griffiths
The art in this book was rendered in gouache, graphite powder and cut paper.
The text was set in Circular Pro.

Printed in China

www.penguinrandomhouse.ca

1   2   3   4   5   26   25   24   23   22

Penguin
Random House
tundra | TUNDRA BOOKS

WHEELS, NO WHEELS

Shannon McNeill

tundra

A tractor has wheels.

A llama has no wheels.

A bike has wheels.

A cat has no wheels.

A skateboard has wheels.

A turtle has no wheels.

There is the tractor.

Llama will drive it.

There is the bicycle.

Cat will ride it.

There is the skateboard.

Turtle will race it.

Whoa! NO. Animals don't go.

Wait—oh! Animals, don't go!

The gate swings open.

Hit the road!

Llama has wheels!

Cat has wheels!

Turtle has wheels!

Farmer has wheels?

Not really, no.

Farmer walks. Walking is slow.

It's no fun, no way to roll.

Farmer has no wheels.

Here's a friend who walks and rolls.

Ox has wheels!

Farmer has wheels!

All together, off we go

and go and go and go

and GO!

Vrooming, zooming, never stopping.

Up ahead a zebra crossing.

Hit the brakes!

Nobody has wheels.

BEEP! BEEP!

So, wait . . . Chicken has wheels?

Llama has wheels!

Cat has wheels!

Turtle has wheels!

Farmer has wheels!

Ox has wheels!

Chicken has wheels!

Everyone has wheels!